PIRATES of the CARIBBEAN

JACK SPARROW

The Coming Storm

by Rob Kidd

Illustrated by Jean-Paul Orpinas

Based on the earlier life of the character, Jack Sparrow,
created for the theatrical motion picture,
"Pirates of the Caribbean: The Curse of the Black Pearl"
Screen Story by Ted Elliott & Terry Rossio and Stuart Beattie and Jay Wolpert,
Screenplay by Ted Elliott & Terry Rossio,
and characters created for the theatrical motion pictures
"Pirates of the Caribbean: Dead Man's Chest" and
"Pirates of the Caribbean: At World's End"
written by Ted Elliott & Terry Rossio

DISNEP PRESS

New York

Printed in the United States of America

First Edition
9 10

Library of Congress Catalog Card Number: 2005905546

ISBN 1-4231-0018-2

The Coming Storm

I, _Captain_ Jack Sparrow, being recently possessed of a ship, a crew, and a hat, do take it upon me from this day forth to faithfully and truthfully recount our adventures on the high seas and lowly streets in this _Captain's Log_. I carry out this duty in accordance with my position as _Captain_ of the good ship _Barnacle_, and, as befits a _Captain_, I do solemnly swear to write nothing but the Truth about me, my crew, and the events that befall us, no matter how fantastical or grim.

I shall begin with the tale of how I became a _Captain_, how my crew became a Crew, how we began our adventures, and, most important, how I came to wear this Hat. Like many stories of adventure, villainy, and thievery, it began on the Island of Tortuga, in a tavern called the Faithful Bride. . . .

CHAPTER ONE

A dim moon rose over the ocean as the wind blew thickening clouds across the sky. Faint shadows were cast upon the island below: huge, black sailing ships, sea monsters, and other things that haunted the midnight waters seemed to cascade over the hills. Few stars were strong enough to twinkle through the stormy haze. The white sands of the beach were swept into little whirlwinds, shifting the patterns on the sand dunes.

A bad night for sailing.

The few respectable citizens of Tortuga stayed snug in their well-guarded houses. Everyone else—buccaneers, swashbucklers, and cutthroats all—was down at the Faithful Bride, drinking ale and rum.

Between gusts of wind from the gathering storm, the noise from the tavern could be heard a half mile away. Laughing, shouting, and the occasional burst of gunfire echoed through the night as drinkers took up a chanty they all knew:

Yo ho, yo ho, a pirate's life for me!
We kindle and char and inflame and
    ignite—drink up me hearties, yo ho!
We burn up the city, we're really a
    fright—drink up me hearties, yo ho!
Yo ho, yo ho, a pirate's life for me . . .

From outside, the Faithful Bride looked

like nothing more than an oversize shack. It wasn't even built out of proper wood, but from the timbers of wrecked boats. It smelled like a boat, too: tar and salt and seaweed and fish. When a light rain finally began to fall, the roof leaked in a dozen places.

Inside, no one seemed to care about the puddles on the floor. Tankards were clashed together for toasts, clapped on the table for refills, and occasionally thrown at someone's head.

It was crowded this night, every last shoddy chair filled in the candle-lit tavern. *I reckon we have enough old salts here to crew every ship in Port Royal*, the Faithful Bride's young barmaid, Arabella, thought. She was clearing empty mugs off a table surrounded by men who were all hooting at a story. Like everyone in the pub, they were dressed in tattered, mismatched garb common to all the "sailors" of the area: ragged breeches, faded waistcoats, stubbly beards, and the odd sash or belt.

One of them tugged on her skirt, grinning toothlessly.

Arabella rolled her eyes and sighed. "Let me guess," she said, tossing aside her tangled auburn locks. "Ale, ale, ale and . . . oh, probably another ale?"

The sailor howled with laughter. "That's my lass!"

Arabella took a deep breath and moved on to the other tables.

"There's no Spanish treasure left but inland, ye daft sprog," a sailor swore.

"I'm not talkin' about *Spanish* treasure," his friend, the second-rate pirate Handsome Todd said, lowering his voice. There was a gleam in his eye, not yet dulled by drink.

"I'm talkin' about Aztec Gold, from a whole *lost kingdom*. . . ."

Arabella paused and listened in, pretending to pick a mug up off the floor.

"Yer not talking about Stone-Eyed Sam and *Isla Esquelética*?" the sailor replied, skeptically. "*Legend* says Sam 'e had the Sword of Cortés, and 'e cursed the whole island. Aye, I agree with only one part of that story—that it's *legend*. Legend, mate. 'A neat little city of stone and marble—just like them there Romans built,' they say. Bah! Rubbish! Aren't nothing like that in the Caribbean, I can tell you!"

"Forget the blasted kingdom and the sword, it's his *gold* I'm talking about," Handsome Todd spat out. "And *I* can tell you, I *know* it's real. Seen it with my own eyes, I have. It changes hands often, like it's got legs all its own. But there are ways of finding it."

"Ye got a ship, then?" the first sailor said with a leery look in his eyes.

"Aye, a fine little boat, perfect for slipping in and out of port unseen . . ." Handsome Todd began. But then he noticed Arabella, who was pretending to wipe something from the floor with her apron. She looked up and gave him a weak smile.

She looked again at the floor and rubbed fiercely with the edge of her apron. "Blasted men, spillin' their ale," she said.

Handsome Todd relaxed. But he looked around suspiciously as if the other buccaneers, the walls, or the King himself were listening. "Let's go somewhere a bit quieter, then, shall we? As they say, *dead men tell no tales.*"

Arabella cursed and moved away. Usually, no one cared—no one *noticed* if she were there or not. To the patrons of the Bride, she was just the girl who filled the tankards. She had heard hundreds of stories and legends over the years. Each story was almost like being on an adventure.

Almost.

Still, she decided, *not a bad night, considering.* It could have been far worse. A storm often seemed to bring out the worst in an already bad lot of men.

And then, suddenly, the door blew open with gale force.

A crash of lightning illuminated the person in the doorway. It was a stranger, wet to the bone. Shaggy black hair was plastered against his head, and the lightning glinted in his eyes. Arabella held her breath—she had never seen anyone like him before.

Then the door slammed shut, and the candlelight revealed an angry, dripping, young man—no older than Arabella. There was silence for a moment. Then the patrons shrugged and returned to their drinks.

The stranger began to make his way through the crowd, eyes darting left and right, up and down like a crow's. He was obviously looking for someone, or some*thing*. His jaw was set in anger.

His hazel eyes lit up for a moment: he must have found what he was looking for. He bent down behind a chair, and reached for something. Arabella stood on her tiptoes to see—it just looked like an old sack. Not at all worth stealing from the infamous pirate who was guarding it.

"Oh, no . . ." Arabella whispered.

The stranger bit his lip in concentration. He stretched his fingers as long and narrow as possible, discreetly trying to reach between the legs of the chair.

Without warning—and without taking

the drink from his lips—the man who sat in the chair rose up, all seven feet and several hundred pounds of him. His eyes were the color of a storm, and they sparked with anger.

The stranger pressed his palms together and gave a quick bow.

"Begging your pardon, Sir, just admiring my . . . I mean *your* fine satchel there," he said, extremely politely.

The pirate roared and brought his heavy tankard down, aiming for the stranger's head.

The stranger grabbed the sack and side-stepped just in time. The mug whistled past his ear . . .

. . . and hit another pirate behind him!

This other pirate wasn't as big, but he was just as irritable. And armed. *And* he thought the stranger was the one who had just hit him in the head with a tankard! The pirate drew a rapier and lunged for the stranger.

The stranger scooted backward, moving out of the way of the deadly blade. His second attacker kept going, falling forward into the table where the giant pirate had been sitting. The rickety table broke under his weight, and drinks, coins, and knives flew into the air. The buccaneers around the table leapt up, drawing their swords and pistols.

It didn't take much to start a barroom brawl in Tortuga.

The Faithful Bride exploded with the sounds of punches, groans, screams, yells and hollers, the clash of cutlasses striking rapiers, and the snap of wood as chairs were broken over heads. All this, in addition to the sound of the crashing thunder and the

leaking ceiling that began to pour down on the brawling patrons.

The stranger was caught in the middle of it. And to make matters worse, the giant pirate was still after him.

The huge pirate drew his sword and swung it at the stranger. The stranger leapt up onto the chair behind him, the blade slicing the air where he had just stood.

"That's a bit close, mate," the stranger said. He jumped off the chair again and kicked at one of its legs, causing it to flip up into the air and land in his hands.

The giant swung again, but the stranger held the chair like a shield, blocking every strike. Bits of wood flew off the chair where the blade hit.

Another pirate dove for the stranger— or maybe for someone behind him, it was hard to tell at this point. The stranger leaned out of the way, just barely avoiding the collision, and his attacker toppled into the giant pirate.

With the giant now otherwise engaged, the stranger hoisted the sack onto his shoulder, turned around and surveyed the scene behind him. What was—for pirates—a fairly quiet night of drinking, had turned into yet another bloody and violent brawl like the others he'd seen in his day. He couldn't resist grinning.

"Huh. Not a *single* bruise on me," he said out loud. "Not one blasted scratch on *Jack Sparrow*."

Then someone smashed a bottle against a timber above his head. The giant had risen behind him, surprisingly quiet for such a large man. Jack swung around to see him and began to back away.

"*You'll just be giving me that sack now, boy,*"

the pirate said in a deadly voice, holding the broken bottle before him and pointing it at Jack.

"Uh . . ." Jack looked around, but he was surrounded by the fight on all sides, still blocked from the door.

"Good Sir . . ." he began, hoping something would come to him. But before he could think of a way out of this one, the giant roared and bolted forward.

A hand grabbed Jack by the collar and yanked him out of the way. But it happened so quickly that the giant kept running and crashed right into a group of a half-dozen pirates who were battering each other along the far wall. There was a crack of wood, a crash of glass, and a blast of rolling thunder from the storm outside. The angry pirates all turned toward the not-so-gentle giant and pounced on him.

Arabella kept a very firm grip on Jack's collar as she pulled him quickly through the crowd, ducking and avoiding the brawling sailors. And *Jack* kept a very firm grip on the sack. *His* sack.

After a few more near misses, Jack and Arabella staggered out the back door and into the stormy tropical night.

CHAPTER TWO

*I*t was raining much harder now, and the wind had picked up incredible speed. Jack and the barmaid were in an alley behind the tavern, and the slight overhang wasn't keeping them dry. He turned to thank the girl who had saved him, but before he could, she threw him up against the side of the Faithful Bride.

"How *dare* ye start a fight in my father's tavern?" She placed her hands on her hips and her brown eyes flashed. "Couldn't ye do your pickpocketing somewhere *else* tonight?

Someplace nicer, whose patrons wouldn't *wreck* the place?" She pushed him against the wall and stepped back.

Jack brushed himself off, straightening the wrinkles in his coat. "Now listen here, lassie, I am *not* a thief. I didn't come here by choice. And I wasn't pickpocketing." Jack waved the sack in Arabella's face. "Capitan 7-foot-beastie in there stole my sack here, and I was simply reclaiming my property. So if my gratitude is worthless to you, I'll just gather up my things, *not* say 'thank you' for being so inhospitable, and be on my merry way. Savvy?"

Jack lifted his head up and started to walk. But Arabella grabbed his arm and threw him up against the wall again.

"Do you have any idea who you've taken that sack from—whether it's yours or not?" she asked.

"No. And truth be told, I do not care," Jack said, wrestling free from Arabella's grip.

"That was Captain *Torrents*, you idiot," Arabella said, slapping Jack upside the head. Jack looked blank.

"The infamous and the dreaded . . . ?" Arabella said.

"Not ringing any bells," Jack answered.

"The most notorious pirate this side of Hispaniola?" Arabella tried again.

"Oh, wait . . ." Jack said with a sudden look of recognition. Then his face fell again, "Nope. Sorry."

"Well, either way, you're as good as dead, stealing from him."

"Look, I am *not* a crook," Jack said. "This crummy sack here—and what's in it—is all I have. I would have brought more, but storage space for stowaways is very limited."

Arabella rolled her eyes.

"Then," Jack continued, "as is typical on this bloody island, a bloody pirate stole it from me. I don't even bloody remember it happening. The bloke, he got me from behind. But what I *can* tell you is that this here is *my* sack." Jack leapt onto an old barrel and opened the sack. "For instance," he said, digging around in the sack, then pulling out what looked like a stick of wax "this candle here is . . . not mine?" Jack looked at the candle, confused, then tossed it down.

"Surprise," Arabella said sarcastically.

"No, no, no!" Jack said, frustrated. Digging deeper, he pulled out what might have been old underwear. He shivered and tossed them away. After that came what looked like a dried up old rat.

"*Arabella*, by the way," the girl said. Jack did not look up. "The 'lassie' has a name," she continued, "and it's Arabella."

"Jack," Jack grunted, not really paying attention. There was no end to the horrible things in the sack. He threw out something that looked very much like petrified dung.

"Look, sorry I went wild on ye," Arabella said sincerely. "It's just, my father's temper is bad enough as it is. He's going to be in a *frightful* state now, spending the next week fixing up the place. Repairing the chairs and tables that ye helped destroy . . ."

There was a small *thump* as something Jack tossed hit Arabella square in the forehead. She caught it as it fell. It was a heavy coin.

"Thank you," she muttered sarcastically. "This makes up for *everything*."

"Well, it's the only thing in here *worth* anything," Jack said glumly. "My knife, my box, my stash of coins . . ." He looked up at her, bewildered, ". . . it's all gone."

Frustrated and angry, he turned the sack upside down and shook out several apple seeds.

Then something big and heavy fell out of the bottom, hitting the ground with a *thunk*. Jack leapt down to look at it. His eyes lit up as his fingers closed around smooth leather: a scabbard. A *long* scabbard. A sword, any sword, would fetch some nice cash on the black market . . . and this one looked like it had some history to it. He would be rich! Well, if not rich at least he could start to buy back the things he had lost.

Then again, perhaps he would keep it for himself. He didn't have a sword. And anyone who was *anyone* in the Caribbean had a sword. . . .

But as he picked up the scabbard, Jack realized the weight was wrong: much too light to have a sword in it.

Jack groaned and threw the empty scabbard to the ground.

"Blasted pirates!"

He rubbed his eyes with his fingers and sank against the tavern wall, contemplating a bleak—and not-so-well-fed—future.

But *Arabella's* eyes widened as the scabbard tumbled to the ground. Was that a flash of gold?

She picked it up, ignoring Jack's grumbles, and turned it over in her hands. Although it was scratched and covered with dirt, glints of gold and silver still remained worked into the leather, which was sparkling with rain. And she could feel a design embossed on it.

"No, it couldn't be . . ." she breathed. "Get me some light," she ordered.

Normally Jack took orders from no one, least of all an angry tavern owner's daughter, but he heard something in Arabella's voice that caught his attention. Without protest, he took out a little flint-and-tinder kit from his coat pocket and lit the candle stub from the sack. Arabella took the candle and cast its weak light over the leather.

"Look, there—" she said, pointing at the scabbard. There were some words in a language neither of them recognized, abbreviations of some sort, and then some more inscriptions in Spanish. Below that was a strange image of a serpent with feathers, worked in reddish gold. Angular and foreign.

Quetzalcoatl. The Aztec god.

Arabella whistled. "Do ye know what this is?" she asked. Her voice quivered with excitement.

"Worth *lots* of gold?" Jack asked.

"It's the scabbard to the *Sword of Cortés*," she whispered.

Jack's eyes widened.

"This says BELONGING TO HERNÁN. This is the cursed sword that gave Cortés the power to conquer the Aztec empire!" Arabella's eyes shone with excitement. "Legend has it that the sword made him unstoppable in battle. . . . And it gave him strange powers, like convincing the Aztecs that he was a god. The Aztecs believed the god Quetzalcoatl would come back to them someday, and with this sword, Cortés convinced them that's who he was. Legend says the sword holds limited power if the one who possesses it doesn't also have its sheath.

"It also played a part in Cortés's downfall. . . . 'The loss of the scabbard will cause kingdoms to scab over,' the saying goes." She turned the scabbard over in her hands, looking at the worn leather and shining jewels, and shuddered. "It's supposed to be made from the innards of Aztec sacrifices."

"Delightful," Jack said, taking the scabbard from her with his thumb and forefinger. "But how did it get *here*?"

"Stone-Eyed Sam had it last," she said, remembering the conversation she overheard earlier in the tavern.

"What, the pirate captain? The scourge of Panama?" Jack asked.

Arabella nodded. "Years ago. He took the sword and sheath and used them to make himself king of an isolated island. No one knows what happened to him *or* to his loyal subjects. Maybe the fact that the sheath has turned up without the sword has something to do with his downfall."

Jack turned the sheath over in his hands, running his fingers up and down the seams. Fine craftsmanship, he thought. The sword was one of the greatest treasures in all the

Caribbean. Which meant losing half of what made it so powerful would rile up any notorious and fearsome pirate to the point of . . . well . . . Jack didn't really want to think about it.

"So, then," Jack said, "why don't I just go back into the tavern, carefully slip the sack back under what's left of Captain Turnip's chair, apologize, and just be done with it? Sorry to have taken your magic scabbard, sir. Didn't know you were planning to start your own pirate kingdom with it. Good luck with all that! Ta, now."

Arabella shook her head. "You're in big trouble," she said quietly. "Stealing something like this from a pirate like Torrents. You'd better leave Tortuga immediately—or you're a dead man." She turned to go back inside.

"Wait," Jack grabbed her arm. "Come with me."

She blinked at him, droplets of rain hanging from her eyelashes.

"You obviously know *far* more about this sort of legendary stuff than I do, and about all the local 'inhabitants' of these waters. And if anyone saw you helping me back there, you're a dead man, too. Well, woman. Well, girl," he stuttered.

Arabella ignored him, thinking about it.

"And," Jack continued, "think about the *freedom* that would be ours if we had that sword. Freedom and *power*." Though Arabella tried to mask it, Jack could tell from her expression that she was in love with the idea.

"Well . . . I don't really have any *other* plans. . . . Besides working at the Bride for the rest of my life, or until I'm married," she said sadly. "Or until Dad dies from the drink," she added, a little angrier. "I've had little—really *nothing*—here since a nasty pirate sacked the Bride last year, taking my mum with him. A big, fierce, ugly one he was, too. I do miss her, me mum. Dad and I are sure she's . . ." Arabella trailed off.

Jack noticed the look on her face and felt a surge of sympathy.

Arabella looked Jack dead in the eyes. "All right. I'll come with ye. But we play by *my* rules. Hear? Which means no stealing from pirates—or anyone else for that matter— along the way."

"How many times do I have to tell you— I'm not a thief!" Jack protested.

Arabella scowled, then continued, "I know the perfect boat to use. An old, abandoned one in Salty Cove."

Jack shrugged. "Sorry, lass. New here, remember? I have *no* idea where that is. And I don't think it would be very wise of me to ask one of those gents inside for directions."

Arabella thought about it for a moment. Then she pulled a wooden hairpin out of her locks and held the tip of it to Jack's candle flame. When it began to burn, she blew it out, leaving a nice charcoal point. Then she tore a square piece of cloth from her apron, set it against the tavern wall, and proceeded to draw a map for him on it.

Jack watched all of this with wide eyes. "I think I shall be very lucky to have such a . . . *resourceful* mate on board with me," he said, leaning forward and grinning.

"Call me resourceful, but I'm not your mate. We're business partners, and that's all," Arabella said, putting a little X on the spot before handing the crude map off to Jack. "Here, ye lay low for three days. I'll gather supplies—drinking water and food.

Meet me at the boat at *dusk* in *three nights' time*."

"Excellently done, my lady," he said, giving her a quick bow.

"We have our boat. But . . ." she looked lost for a moment, her bout of energy over. The Faithful Bride had been her only home. "Where will we go?"

Jack rolled his eyes. "To get the blasted, cursed sword, of course! You've already said we're as good as dead. How much *deader* would we be if Cortés's missing blade and the powers of a god-king fell into the hands of Captain Torn Pants?"

"*Torrents*," Arabella corrected.

"Whatever."

CHAPTER THREE

*Th*ree days later, several hours after the sun had already set, Arabella was scowling and pacing. Sometimes, she would stop to glare angrily at the roiling sky and impatiently tap her foot. It should have been so easy! An *idiot* could have followed her directions.

The rain hadn't stopped since the night she'd met Jack. The tiny shack on Salty Cove where she was waiting for him leaked worse than her father's tavern, which was really saying something. She chose to move outside, under the eaves, near where their boat was docked. She'd lit three torches to guide them through the stormy night.

The boat was a tiny thing, little more than a fancy fishing vessel. The name BARNACLE was painted gaudily across the stern. But she was seaworthy and the sails looked in good shape. And far more important, she really did seem to be abandoned.

Where is *he?* Arabella wondered with increasing frustration.

Then there was a loud crash in the scrub at the head of the cove.

Arabella put her hand on the dagger she had hidden in her pocket. . . .

"My lady," Jack came falling out of the woods—not at all on the trail Arabella had mapped out—and staggered forward onto the tiny beach. He bowed dramatically.

"I am here. Let us set sail and let the adventure begin."

His shirt was torn at the sleeve, and his hair was a mess. There was something that looked suspiciously like blood on his trousers.

"*Mr. Sparrow*," Arabella breathed, trying not to show her relief. "You're *hours* late! What happened? I thought I gave ye specific instructions. . . ."

"Yes, well," he half-hid his mouth by scratching at his nose and looked away so she couldn't see his eyes. "A number of obstacles, flotsam and jetsam really, nothing important . . . But I'm here, aren't I?"

"You've been in a fight," Arabella sighed, taking his hand and pulling it away from his face. A straight, deep cut went from his cheekbone almost to his mouth.

"I found my sack!" Jack admitted, holding

it up happily. "And though you may not believe this to be possible, being as it was in hands as capable as my own, the map was . . . misplaced."

"Ye *lost* the map," Arabella scolded. "Then how on earth did ye find me?"

"There are any number of ways to reach a desired destination, lassie."

Arabella shook her head grimly and kicked her muddy pile of bags against the barrel she'd rolled all the way there. It had taken most of her spare time to sneak what they needed away from the tavern.

She scowled at Jack, who repositioned his newly found sack on his shoulder. "The point is, I'm here. Tide's rising. Mustn't waste time. Shall we, lassie?" Jack asked, extending his arm toward the boat.

"Call me *'lassie'* again, and ye will be drinking up the tide," Arabella grumbled under her breath as they began to load up the *Barnacle*.

"Halt," a sudden voice rang out.

Jack slumped and sighed. "Oh, *now* what?"

"I am coming with you," the voice continued.

Jack looked up, Standing at the trailhead, one foot placed dramatically on a rock, was a handsome, well-dressed young man. He was about the same age as Jack and Arabella, but that was where the similarities ended. He was tall and broad-shouldered, and he wore an immaculate jacket and a pair of breeches that were cut perfectly to his figure. All his buttons were polished, and an elegant sword hung from his belt.

Jack took the other boy in with a sneer. "Sorry, chap," he began, "this boat is ready to set sail. The crew, meaning Bell here and myself, are no longer accepting passengers. Go home to the pleasant estate you came from and have a nice life."

"I am Fitzwilliam P. Dalton the Third," the young man said, ignoring Jack and striding forward.

"I don't care if you're *Pope* Fitzdalton P. William the *Seventh*." Jack said. "I don't know what you're doing here, but we are very busy sailors with very important things to do. So if you don't mind, we'll just raise the sails, set our course, et cetera, et cetera— all without *you*—and be on our way." He pressed his hands together and gave a mocking bow, then quickly turned on his heel back toward the *Barnacle*.

"Very busy, important sailors?" Fitzwilliam said with badly hidden scorn. He carefully removed from his pocket a piece of cloth and delicately unfolded it.

"The map . . ." Arabella whispered, recognizing it at once, and glaring at Jack.

Fitzwilliam haughtily read aloud: "'Meet Arabella at this spot at dusk, in order to commandeer boat, find Sword of Cortés, eliminate Captain Torniquet, acquire the perfect hat, become Captain, rule entire Caribbean, live Happily Ever After.'"

"Oh, Jack," Arabella said, clearly embarrassed.

"I suppose I have not arrived too late for the 'hat' part," Fitzwilliam added, looking meaningfully at Jack's ragged hair.

"Yes, yes, so what," Jack said impatiently. "So I have a life plan. What do *you* have? Well, besides a fancy silk suit that you seem to like to wear in pouring rain while wading through mud." Jack turned to Arabella and whispered, "The pastimes of these aristos are so sick and odd . . . yet strangely intriguing."

"I have decided to accompany you," Fitzwilliam announced grandly, and produced his own kit bag. It was much nicer than anything Arabella or Jack had, new leather and probably full of nice, expensive things.

Jack opened his mouth to protest, but Arabella silenced him.

"Why?" she asked, intrigued. "Ye're obviously wealthy and . . . don't have the need *we* do for treasure. A man in your position can do anything he wants—ye don't have to sneak away from your family for adventure. At least not the way I do, ye know," she glared at Jack, "me being a 'lassie' and all."

"*Au contraire*, my lady." Fitzwilliam bowed. "As the eldest son of the Earl of Dalton, I am *precisely* bound by the same sort of family rules you are. Perhaps more so. We came from England less than a month ago, when my father decided to expand his holdings into the New World. Since then, I have been forced to do nothing but attend balls and cotillions of other English families."

"Oh, sounds *dreadful*," Jack muttered.

"You have no *idea*," Fitzwilliam said with some heat. "Regardless, I am expected to choose one of the English ladies I meet and marry her within the next year. I am forbidden from entering the naval service or pursuing any career other than what my father chooses for me. Which is, namely, continuing the family Dalton. Which means chaperoned walks with stupid rich girls, dinners with my father's friends—who are three times my age—and acres and acres of banana trees."

"Sounds dreadful," Arabella echoed Jack.

"I'd take drunken old sailors over bunches of bananas any day."

"So, when I found this, it was a sign." Fitzwilliam held up the map. "My escape. My destiny. My adventure."

"Your *exit*," Jack said quickly. "The high seas are no place for a wellborn fop like yourself. Run along now, Fitzy. Bye-bye."

"Oh, come on, Jack, he might be useful," Arabella whispered. "He can afford supplies when we run out. And it would be handy to have another pair of strong arms aboard."

"You seem to be man enough for the job at hand," Jack said.

"Thanks," Arabella said. "I think."

"It matters not," Fitzwilliam interrupted. "I *am* coming."

"No. You're. Not," Jack said.

The three stood there quietly for a moment. The rain continued to pour all around them. A wind rattled some of the rigging on the *Barnacle*.

Fitzwilliam paused. Then, after a moment, he said, "I challenge you to a duel. I win, you let me come with you. I lose, I leave and tell no one what I have seen here, or anything of your plans."

"Oh, Fitzy, I would *love* to," Jack said, not really sounding regretful. "But, as it happens, I have yet to acquire the sword I really want. No sword, no duel. No boarding the ship for you. *So sorry.*"

"Oh, that's not a problem," Arabella said, a mischievous look on her face. "When I was cleaning out the boat I found a half dozen rapiers stored in a chest. . . ." She went over to the *Barnacle* and triumphantly pulled out a cheap, rusty old sword. She tossed it to Jack. "Here ye go."

"Thank you, *my lady*," Jack said through

gritted teeth. He caught the sword easily and tested its weight. It wasn't very well-made.

Fitzwilliam pulled out his own weapon, a beautifully balanced rapier, which made a clean swoosh in the air as he saluted his opponent.

"Show-off," Jack muttered.

Then they leapt forward.

Their blades met with a loud clang. Sparks scattered on the dark beach.

Jack moved energetically forward and backward, lunging and dipping and posturing. Fitzwilliam barely moved at all, using short quick swipes of his wrist to parry his opponent's attacks. When he did move in, it was with precise, swift, controlled footwork.

"This is going to be a massacre," Arabella said, feeling a little sorry for Jack. Fitzwilliam obviously had the advantage of years of training, probably from some great English

arms master. The nobleman was also almost a full head taller than Jack, and muscled where Jack was slender.

Jack had no shortage of enthusiasm, however. And he was full of little tricks like leaping up on rocks and driftwood to avoid the tip of Fitzwilliam's sword.

But all of his talents combined were no match for the would-be next Earl of Dalton.

Grimacing in concentration, Fitzwilliam redoubled his attack. He lunged forward with all his strength. Jack avoided the worst blow by throwing himself to the ground and rolling backward . . .

. . . but when he sat up, rapier in his hands, Fitzwilliam was already above him, his sword at Jack's throat.

"Yield," Fitzwilliam commanded, grinning in triumph.

Jack frowned. For a moment it looked like

he was going to refuse. He finally sighed and dropped his blade.

"All right. All right. You don't have to act all superior about it," he muttered.

"Ah," Fitzwilliam sheathed his rapier with a satisfying *snik* and put his hand out to help Jack up. "A gracious loser as well as a busy and important sailor. I see I am blessed in the capabilities of my shipmates."

Jack batted Fitzwilliam's hand away and leapt up by himself. "Fitzy is quite annoying, eh?" he whispered to Arabella.

She didn't entirely disagree. Strong and capable—and handsome—he might be, but Fitzwilliam P. Dalton III definitely also had the makings of a first-class snob.

"Well, then we're a team," Arabella said, putting her hand out. For the first time Fitzwilliam looked unsure, taking her hand hesitantly. He had probably never shaken hands with a woman before. Jack put his hand on top of the other two, grinning with sudden enthusiasm.

"To adventure!" he toasted.

"To adventure," Arabella repeated, grinning.

"Yes, to adventure," Fitzwilliam said, slowly and seriously.

". . . and of course," Jack added, smiling, "to treasure . . . and freedom!"

CHAPTER FOUR

$\mathcal{B}$y the crew's third day at sea, a blinding sun shone brightly against the blue sky. The weather had steadily improved the farther they sailed from Tortuga. This should have been good news, but nothing moved under the sun's heat: the sea was as flat as glass. There were no ripples of fish, no movement of the sails. No breeze at all.

It was very, very hot, and the *Barnacle* was in the middle of the sea, with no land in sight. The crew had only a little drinking

water left, which might last one more day—
if they rationed it very carefully.

The crew sat wilted and unmoving on the
deck. Fitzwilliam had even finally taken off
his fine blue jacket—not very proper for a
nobleman. Jack had no issues with modesty
and opened his shirt as widely as he could.

Fitzwilliam didn't bother hiding his disgust with the situation.

"It has been days now," he said. "Two of
those days without a single wind or any idea
of where we are."

"We know that, Fitz," Arabella said
crossly. She had pinned up her hair to keep
cool, but rivulets of sweat still ran down her
neck.

"I thought ye two were *sailors*," Arabella
challenged.

"Well, I know *I* am," Jack protested.
Arabella and Fitzwilliam just stared. "A

sailor," Jack continued, and so did the stares, ". . . of sorts," Jack finished, before quickly turning away.

"What about *ye*," Arabella said, throwing a compass at Fitzwilliam's chest. "'Oh, me father the earl taught me all about reading maps and charts and latitudes and the rest!'" she said in a snooty, mocking tone.

"If we *had* a map, I *could* read it," Fitzwilliam growled.

"Oh, yes, they are so very easy to come by, those secret maps to pirate kingdoms," Jack said sarcastically. "Or they would be, if there really *were* a blasted pirate kingdom . . ." he added under his breath, sneering at Arabella.

"And what's *that* supposed to mean?" Arabella demanded. "I told ye I *thought* Stone-Eyed's *Isla Esquelética* was probably one of the smaller Leeward Islands. I never claimed to know *exactly* where he landed!"

"You sounded awful sure back at the cove," Jack said sternly.

"Oh, hang the both of ye!" Arabella snarled in a very unladylike way, and turned her back on Jack and Fitzwilliam.

Jack sighed. He took off his bandana and mopped his face with it. As a gesture of goodwill he offered it to Fitzwilliam, but the nobleman's son just gave him a look of disgust. Jack shrugged and put it back on, tucking in a stray bit of hair that the breeze kept blowing out of place.

He stopped suddenly, realizing something:

A *breeze* kept blowing his hair out of place. A breeze!

He licked his finger and held it up, turning around to determine the breeze's source.

He turned to the southeast, the direction of the very faint wind.

"Fitz, give me your glass," he demanded.

Too hot and tired to argue, the other boy opened his kit and carefully pulled out a spyglass, a gift from his father, his most prized possession. It was made of what looked like brass and copper, but could just as well have been gold. It had lenses made in Holland by the finest craftsmen.

Jack treated the small telescope far less gently, opening it with a snap that made Fitzwilliam flinch. Jack held the glass to his eye and looked to the south.

"What is it, Jack?" Arabella asked, forgetting her anger.

"A wind, finally," he answered.

"Huzzah!" Fitzwilliam exclaimed.

Both Jack and Arabella stared at him dubiously.

Fitzwilliam shifted uncomfortably, "I believe I meant, yo, ho, ho! Wind! Um, yar," he said quite unnaturally, clearing his throat.

In the distance, Jack could see a fast-moving gray curtain of showers. As he lowered the glass, the wind was already rising around them. "And there's rain with it, too."

"Well, that is excellent news. We shall not die of thirst, then . . ." Fitzwilliam said. Then the first clouds began to darken the skies overhead.

"No, we certainly will not die . . . of thirst," Jack said, biting his lip. Eerie, sharp squawks suddenly sounded overhead. Jack looked up to see flocks of gulls, pelicans, and other sea birds covering the darkening sky, fleeing the approaching storm.

The crew was silent for a few minutes, watching both sea and sky churn before them. A light drizzle began, peppering the ocean with tiny ripples. The sky became gradually darker, as if some great lamp in the heavens were being turned down slowly. The unruly surf became more violent, carelessly tossing the ship about.

"Where did it come from?" Arabella murmured. "I mean, it seems so strange, the sky, the sea . . . they were so still a moment ago."

"Where it comes from does not matter," Jack said. "It's where it's going that should be of concern to us. Especially as it seems headed directly for the mighty *Barnacle*."

"Come, now, it is probably no more than a squall," Fitzwilliam said, squinting to keep his eyes shielded from the increasingly heavy rain. "If we are able to stay afloat, it shall all be over in an hour or two. We shall get through this easily."

As though in response, a tremendous crash of thunder, louder than any cannon fire the crew had ever heard, rocked the ship. Unimaginably long forks of lightning flashed

all around them, and a huge, swelling wave swept over the deck, drenching the shipmates.

"Help me grab the line," Jack ordered. "Reef the sails immediately."

"*Lower* the sails? But we finally have a wind!" Fitzwilliam protested.

Jack stepped up to him, "Of course, we have winds. How pleasant and how convenient for us. They'll just get caught in the sails and push us on our merry way toward *Isla Esquelética*," his voice became sterner, "or they'll tip this boat over like a child's toy. Savvy?"

Fitzwilliam understood. The two boys lowered the sails and made the rigging fast. Arabella battened down the hatches as best she could. Her almost encyclopedic knowledge of pirates, legends of the sea, and history contained almost nothing about the actual practice of sailing. She acted on instinct, tying up loose rope and other things on the deck, and went below to secure what few personal items they had lying around the sleeping quarters.

Soon the storm was hitting them full force. Jack and Fitzwilliam had just tied down the lowermost sail and made the boom secure when the fierce storm delivered them a huge punch. Wind screamed around the rigging. The rain became a flood of water pouring from a pitch-black sky. Above, clouds roiled and swirled, mirroring the waves below.

The *Barnacle* pitched wildly as Jack and Fitzwilliam tried to turn the boat to run with the storm. But even with Arabella adding her strength, the wheel spun out of control, and the rudder pulled away from them.

Water poured over the deck in flash floods

so severe that the crew couldn't keep their footing. The three novice sailors were thrown from railing to railing as the *Barnacle* rocked in the storm.

"It's no good!" Fitzwilliam shouted. "The *Barnacle* is being tossed around like a toy!"

"Fitz, grab your axe! Help me take the mainmast down!" Jack yelled.

"You *are* mad!" Fitzwilliam shouted.

"Just listen to me. You can tell me I'm wrong later, when we are *not* dead," Jack yelled. "I'll lower it down from the other side. . . . Bell," he turned to her, "I need you to make a sea anchor—grab anything heavy you can, like a barrel or Fitzy's bag, whatever—something that will give us drag. Tie a rope to it firmly and feed it off the aft end. Got it?"

"Aye, aye," she said and ran off.

Jack put his knife in his teeth and scurried

up the mast like a monkey, clinging tightly as the wind tried to push him off. He cut down the rigging as he went, allowing it, and the sails, to fall to the deck. At the very top, he grabbed the last remaining rope and used it to swing down, letting the slack out as he went.

"Now! Fitz!" he yelled.

Fitzwilliam did as he was told, hacking at the mast as if it were a tree. Standing on the pitching deck, Jack braced himself with the rope. When the long timber finally began to topple, he let the rope out, easing the mast down as best he could. It still smashed a hole in the deck where it fell. Fitzwilliam barely leapt out of the way in time.

"It's all done, Jack!" Arabella shouted over the roar of the storm. "But why did ye need to do that? Aren't we as good as dead now?"

"We were top heavy," Jack shouted back. "The wind was still catching at the mast. But that danger is past. Now, hold fast to the wheel!"

Two at a time, they held the wheel to steady the ship, while the third went below and bailed the water out using buckets.

And still the storm beat down.

After hours of wet misery spent just keeping the *Barnacle* afloat, the clouds and the rain swept on. Within a few short minutes, it was as if there had never been a storm at all. The sun shone and fish leapt out of the water.

Jack's plan had worked. The *Barnacle* was upright, though it had really taken a beating.

And then a tan-and-green line appeared on the blue horizon before them.

"Land!" Jack shouted, looking through

Fitzwilliam's spyglass. "We must have been pushed here by the wind before we anchored but could not see anything through the storm!"

"Let us heave to and look for water," Fitzwilliam said. "Not," he added quickly to Arabella who was wringing out her skirts, "that the use of our fresh water didn't make for a great anchor."

"It was the *only* heavy barrel we had," she snapped. "And you're free to drink the rainwater on the deck, Master Dalton."

"Now, mates," Jack interrupted, "let's get that mast back up and raise what sail we can. There's a good amount of rope below deck that could secure it, at least for now."

CHAPTER FIVE

Swept along by a strong current, and helped by their wobbly mast and make-shift sails, the *Barnacle* made it to the island by the following morning. The island was barely a few miles across. It was clearly uninhabited. There were no columns of smoke promising any towns or docks.

The crew laid anchor, jumped into the water, and waded to the shore.

"Maybe there will be a spring or a stream on that hill there," Arabella pointed at a rise in the distance as they climbed out onto the beach. It looked like the scrub turned into a thick, lush jungle inland—a good indication of water.

"Absolutely!" Fitzwilliam said cheerfully. "You should go back and wait in the boat and Jack and I will seek it out."

Arabella stepped on Fitzwilliam's foot as she marched past him up the beach and away from the boat. Jack sighed.

"But there might be dangerous natives or beasts!" Fitzwilliam protested, as Arabella ignored his warnings.

"I see only *one* beast around here," Arabella muttered, glaring at Fitzwilliam as she hiked up her skirts and stepped into the brush.

The weather on the island was very hot. Weighed down with leather flasks and water bags, it was slow going for the three adventurers.

"Please, Arabella," Fitzwilliam said when she stumbled. "At least let me take *one* of those bags from you. You're too weak to carry all that."

"Oh, Bell," Jack whined. "Please let him act as your manservant if it's the only way to shut him up."

"Your mother must be very proud," Arabella grunted at Fitzwilliam as she handed her bags over to the strong young man.

"My mother died when I was nine," Fitzwilliam said, a fierce look on his face. "I *hope* she would be proud of the man I became."

"Oh, I'm so sorry," Arabella said sincerely, remembering her own mother. "I didn't know. . . ."

Fitzwilliam stared into the distance sadly. "It was after she died that my father first started looking into expanding his holdings into the New World. It was like he wanted to cut himself off from England and his old life forever."

"Talk as we walk, mates. Chop-chop. No time to lose here," Jack said, ignoring Fitzwilliam's story and pushing through the jungle.

"He married my elder sisters off immediately," Fitzwilliam continued, "to the sons of people he knew who had already moved here to the New World. Some of them we had never even met," Fitzwilliam said to Arabella, whacking a bush aside with his sword. "Not since we were all children, anyway."

Jack, who was in front of them, rolled his eyes at Fitzwilliam's story.

Fitzwilliam paused for a moment, wrestling a small tree out of the way. "Anna, my favorite sister, was abducted by pirates on the voyage over to meet her husband, and I have not seen her since."

"Blazes! I know that pain all too well myself. My mum was taken by pirates, too. If you're like me, ye didn't really have much reason to stick around once ye got here," Arabella said softly.

"No, not really," Fitzwilliam agreed, a hard edge to his voice.

"In the name of all that's blessed and blasted," Jack blurted out, "can we *please* call the curtain on this dismal drama and focus on the matter at hand?"

Arabella and Fitzwilliam looked at Jack, more disappointed than angry. Jack brushed himself off and cleared his throat. "Very well, then, carry on," Jack said.

*I*f the sun was hot the morning they landed, it was nothing compared to midday. The crew finished what little rainwater they had collected in their flasks and still saw no sign of any freshwater on the island. Fitzwilliam tried to hide it, but he began to cough with thirst. Arabella fell once, though she claimed she had stumbled on a root.

Jack looked worriedly at his companions. None of them would be able to go on much longer. A stupid, terrible way to end an adventure.

"Come on," Jack said with a forced smile. "It looks like the brush thins out up ahead. It'll be cool and shady under those trees, and we can rest there for a while."

Arabella nodded wearily.

As Jack pushed the bushes aside and led his two mates into the clearing, he was thrilled—and a little surprised—to see that it was exactly what he had told them—cool, shady, nice, soft grass to relax on. And he was just as surprised to see in the clearing two boys, working over what looked like a makeshift raft.

"Well, *bonswa* and *bienvenue!*" the first kid said. "Look what we got here, Tumen! New friends—and maybe even a way off this island!"

CHAPTER SIX

*T*he two boys stood up to face the crew of the *Barnacle*. The one who had spoken was taller, with dark skin and curly brownish-red hair that matched his freckles. There was a mischievous but friendly look in his green eyes.

"Welcome to our deserted island," he said, bowing theatrically. "I am Jean, and this is my friend, Tumen."

Tumen gave a very slight nod. He was short, with glossy black hair, a sharp nose, and tanned skin. Arabella and Jack exchanged a look; he was definitely native, but dressed in the same ragged sailor clothes as Jean.

"I'm Jack Sparrow," Jack said. "This is Arabella and Fitz."

Jean picked a water bag off a stump and offered it to Arabella, who drank hungrily.

"You were caught in the same cursed storm, huh?" Jean asked. "Tumen and I were on the *Seraph*. I think we are the only survivors—the English don't teach their sailors to swim so well."

"That's terrible," Arabella said, taking a deep breath, wiping her mouth, and handing the water bag over to Fitzwilliam.

"It's pretty hot and not so nice around here. But still, this is not the worst place to have washed up," Jean pointed to the island around them. "Coconuts for eating, a freshwater spring up that way. And there is plenty of lumber. We're building a raft to try to get back to our home port." He pointed to the pile of crudely chopped driftwood logs. Nearby lay several coiled lengths of vine, to lash the logs together.

"There's more water, then?" Fitzwilliam asked, as he handed the water bag to Jack who turned it upside down—not a drop left!

"There's as much as you want, my friend." Jean laughed. "If you do not mind the . . . *ambience*."

Tumen held up what looked like a human bone.

Jack choked.

"Oh, my goodness," Arabella breathed.

"Plenty more where that came from, too," Jean said darkly. "That is why we have been sticking close to the beach."

Jack, Arabella, and Fitz stared at the bone in silence.

HSSSSSSSSSSSSSSST!

Arabella screamed, and Fitzwilliam jumped back as a furry, gray, hideous . . . thing . . . burst into the clearing. It leapt onto a stump, hissing and yowling and baring ugly little yellow fangs.

Tumen gave a faint smile. Jean laughed.

"What in the Greater Antilles is *that*?" Jack asked.

"*That* is Constance." Jean knelt down on one knee and scratched the monster delicately under the chin. It calmed down and began behaving like an actual cat. A scrawny, mangy, scary cat with wild yellow eyes and a crooked tail.

"You managed to save that cat along with yourselves?" Jack said, sneering over at the nasty little creature. "*Why?*"

73

"Constance isn't *just* a cat," Jean said proudly. "She is my sister."

The crew of the *Barnacle* looked at each other.

"Your sister," Jack said dubiously.

"She *is* my sister. Well, she was. I mean she is, but she's not like she used to be. See, she's under a curse, cast by the mystic Tia Dalma herself."

"Was the spell cast because she was this vile in her previous incarnation?" Jack asked.

"Aw, poor thing," Arabella said, reaching a hand out to the cat. "Let me just—*ow!*"

Constance hissed again and swiped out with a paw full of long, yellow claws. They left three bloody scratches on the back of Arabella's hand.

"You little . . ." Arabella said, pulling her hand away.

"*Definitely* nasty," Jack said.

"What a little brute," Fitzwilliam said in wonder, offering Arabella a handkerchief. She took it and wrapped it around her hand. Constance growled a little. Then she leapt off the post and walked away sulkily, her crooked tail high in the air.

"She's just been through a lot," Jean protested.

Jack rolled his eyes. "All right. Now that we have *all* been introduced—and I assume there isn't anyone else? No nephews turned into rats, no second cousins turned into rabid dogs? No? Well then, would you mind leading us to this spring you mentioned?"

"With pleasure," Jean grinned. "Follow me!"

CHAPTER SEVEN

The crew of the *Barnacle* followed Jean and Tumen—and Constance—along a well-worn path. It led deeper into the island, directly toward the jungle. Soon, small trees shielded the crew from the sun. With the shade and the promise of a good drink of water, Jack, Arabella, and Fitzwilliam felt their spirits renewed.

"Aren't ye a bit wee, lad, I mean to serve on a ship?" Arabella asked Jean curiously. He and Tumen both were a couple years younger than the rest of them—thirteen at the oldest.

"Not a private merchant ship—" Jean gave an elaborate shrug, not missing a step through the undergrowth. "As the song says, 'there are a lot of ships in the Caribbean. . . .' And a lot of rum and sugar that sails the high seas. Tumen and I have an advantage: we are reliable, we are not married, and unlike the *old* salts—we do not *drink*." He grinned at Arabella who found herself smiling back.

Behind them, Fitzwilliam walked close to Jack.

"Are you going to tell them of our vessel, the *Barnacle*?"

"Of course I am," Jack said in a dismissive huff, obviously *not* having thought about it before. "They need a ship, and we need a crew."

"Assuming they even want to join us, are

you sure that's wise? We do not know anything about them, really." Fitzwilliam glanced toward Tumen and Constance. They were both bringing up the rear, walking as silently as ghosts.

Constance flattened her ears and bared her fangs at Fitzwilliam. He shuddered.

"Well, besides the odd stroke of luck that saved our tails on this most recent mission, we don't know anything about *navigating*, either," Jack pointed out. "Or did you miss the bit where we got lost and wound up in a hurricane? These lads know what they're doing. We'll never find the Sword of Cortés without decent navigators."

"All right, but if anything happens, I will take Jean. You take Tumen." Fitzwilliam tapped the pommel of his sword.

"And Arabella gets the cat," Jack said, adding, "hardly a fair fight . . . poor Bell!"

"Ah—here we are," Jean declared. "Drink up, *mes amis!*"

Beyond what looked like just another patch of scrubby trees was a secluded, cool little nook. A rocky overhang shaded a series of clear pools fed by a spring that bubbled up like a fountain.

Arabella immediately fell to the ground and began drinking handfuls of the cold water.

Jean laughed. "The pool below the spring is just as clean—and much easier to fill your bags with."

"And have you suffered any ill effects as a result of drinking this?" Fitzwilliam asked.

"It's been a full day now, and *non*," Jean said with a shrug. He sat down and rested his hands on his knees. Tumen stood quietly nearby. "But what are you going to do, now that you have water? Please tell me that the three of you have a ship to go back to. . . ."

"As a matter of fact, we do," Jack answered proudly. "The mighty *Barnacle* survived the storm. We just need to strengthen the mast, and she's set to sail."

"Where is the rest of your crew?" Tumen asked.

"Ah, you're looking at it," Jack said, grinning.

Jean laughed again. "*Mon dieu*—mighty, you said your ship was?"

"Can you take us to our port?" Tumen asked.

"Aye," Jack said, trying to think through all the angles quickly. As much as he didn't want to admit that Fitzwilliam was right, it *did* seem a little too early to invite these two—three, rather—with open arms. "We could. If it's on our way . . ."

"Oh! Disgusting!" Arabella shouted suddenly, trying not to shriek.

It first appeared as if Constance were making amends, trotting up to Arabella's injured hand and mewing a little. But instead of licking it or purring, the cat daintily dropped a human finger bone into the grass before her.

Jack looked curious. "Where are all these coming from?" he asked.

"Up the path, there," Jean said pointing. "We can take a closer look, if you'd like."

When they had all turned to go and she thought no one was looking, Arabella glared at the cat. "This isn't over," she told her.

The path they now followed was barely more than an indentation in the dirt. It went around the back of the spring and up the rise behind it. From there, it climbed slowly toward the jungle. Halfway up the hill, they could see over the jungle vines to the beach. Jack squinted, trying to find the *Barnacle* on the water. It was bobbing against large swells.

"What?" he said, puzzled. The perfect sea they had sailed in on was gone. The surf was growing rough, and to the north the sky was growing cloudy again.

"Not that storm again!" Arabella sighed. "It's like it's *following* us."

"That is very strange," Jean said. "It seemed to have gone past us. To the north, as it should have. I've never seen a tropical storm come *from* the north."

A bent and gnarled beach pine shivered in the rising breeze, making creepy whispery noises as the wind blew through its needles.

"It's headed right toward us. Again," Jack confirmed. He looked back at the beach, then forward into the green, tropical center of the island. "We should press on—faster," he decided. "We'll be safer under the cover of the jungle."

No one disagreed.

They plunged forward, and in a few minutes they were under curvy palms and thick vines, leaving the scrub behind. The breeze blew harder, making the giant leaves rattle against each other. Except for the rustling leaves, it was completely silent. No insects chirped or birds called. Not a single animal was there to be seen or heard.

"I wish I could wear trousers," Arabella complained, carefully lifting her skirt as she stepped over a log.

"You would make a very pretty pirate," Jean said, grinning. "But how did your friends let you aboard? Women are bad luck on ships, you know."

"So are *cats*," Arabella shot back, shaking her fist at him where Constance's scratches still bled a little.

"*Touché*," Fitzwilliam said, smiling for what seemed like the first time.

"Oh, you speak French, too?" Jean asked.

"*Oui*. French, German, Latin, and Greek," Fitz said proudly.

"Ah. Excellent. *Greek*," Jack said. "No doubt *that* will be useful when we come up against angry natives on this island."

"*Nretamaj ri qach'ab'äl MA JUN saqwinäq itzel*," Tumen muttered.

"What did he say?" Arabella asked, curious.

Jean just shrugged. "It wasn't French Creole."

Soon the path grew a little wider, and flat stones appeared underfoot, pushing their way out of the moss at regular intervals, almost as if the path had once been a paved road.

At first, it was hard to see all the bones. They were old and dry and splintered, like pieces of driftwood or fallen branches from a long-dead tree.

Further on, larger pieces of skeletons began to litter the ground. Whole skulls and rib cages poked out of the dirt. Old, rotted clothing and leather belts hung limply from thin bony frames, slowly being reclaimed by the jungle.

"I wonder what killed them all," Arabella said in wonder. "There are no marks on the bones. It doesn't seem like there was a war, or any sort of battle. They just seem to have . . . died."

"There are so many," Fitzwilliam said, sounding a lot less brave than he probably would have liked.

"Well," Jack said flatly. "Very exciting. Our first meeting with the natives. I wonder if they really do speak Greek."

Just then Constance hissed and ran ahead, disappearing around the bend.

"CONSTANCE!" Jean yelled. He ran forward, pushing Jack aside.

"Maybe you shouldn't—" Jack began.

But Jean had already vanished into the underbrush.

"Blasted kids . . ." Jack said through gritted teeth, running after him.

"Constance, get down from there," he heard Jean saying. There was an unpleasant scraping noise—like claws scratching at rock. "NO! Constance, NO!"

When Jack turned the corner, he saw Jean standing there by himself. There was a strange, surprised look on his face.

The ground was giving way beneath Jean's

feet. Large boulders creaked and shuddered, then rolled forward and down, disappearing.

Jean pitched down after them, into the darkness.

"Jean!" Tumen yelled, running forward. Jack, Arabella, and Fitzwilliam followed close behind.

They all stopped and stared at the scene below them.

It wasn't a pit, it was a small valley, just below them. What they were standing on was actually the top of a city wall—the boulders had been part of a turret. Below them stretched the sunken remains of an ancient city. Crumbling houses, dust-covered boulevards neatly laid out in stone, wells gone dry long ago. And it was littered with hundreds upon hundreds of skeletons.

"Well, good day, City of the Dead," Jack said, smiling.

CHAPTER EIGHT

*I*n the valley below, Jean was rubbing his head. Otherwise, he didn't look too badly hurt.

"I'm all right," he called up. Then he turned and saw where he was. A lonely wind blew, whistling and moaning through the ancient structures. It raised an eerie dust cloud over the empty streets, scattering bones as it went.

"This place is accursed," Fitzwilliam said grimly. "We should not tarry here."

"No, wait! Jack," Arabella cried. "'A city neat and well-designed, like the Romans built.' A pirate paradise!" she said excitedly. "And look!" She pointed at what looked like a variation of an Aztec pyramid in the dead center of the city. Then, noticing a coin by her feet, she bent to pick it up. An *S* and a crude hieroglyph of an eye were carved on its face. "This is the mark of Captain Stone-Eyed Sam! This is *his* island, Jack! This is the pirate kingdom we were looking for!"

Jack took in the scene and smiled.

"You were *looking* for this place?" Jean asked from below.

"We are *looking* for the Sword of Cortés," Jack explained.

Jean and Tumen each muttered something in his own language. Constance hissed at nothing in particular.

"But, how is this possible?" Fitzwilliam

asked. "The island we just *happen* to land on after the storm just *happens* to be the one we were looking for?"

"Well, that's luck for you," Jack said with a smile, and began clambering down the wall. Tumen followed.

"It's not luck. We're here *because* we were looking for it," Arabella said. "The sword—or the scabbard—clearly drew us to this place."

"Stuff and nonsense," Fitzwilliam retorted. But he hurried down after them anyway.

Jack tried to keep his and everyone else's spirits up as they explored the city, but it was difficult. Even the promise of the Sword of Cortés wasn't enough to erase the horror of the things they saw. Since they had no idea where the sword might be, they had to look everywhere.

They saw the skeleton of a washerwoman still bent over a tub, the clothes inside long-dry and eaten away. What was once a tavern—chillingly similar to the Faithful Bride—was populated with dead patrons, mugs of dust in bony hands.

Humans weren't the only dead in the city, either. There were pens of cattle, a dog right on the heels of a cat, rows of delicate bird bones on the edges of houses. And behind it all, the wind groaned, blowing grit into Jack and the crew's eyes and teeth.

"What could possibly have happened here?" Fitzwilliam wondered. "Plague? A fire?"

"It was a curse," Tumen muttered.

"The Sword of Cortés," Jack said. "As soon as Stone-Eyed Sam lost the scabbard, his kingdom went to ruin."

"'The loss of the scabbard will cause

kingdoms to scab over,'" Arabella muttered to herself, repeating the same line she'd heard at the inn.

"This is just where the commoners lived," Jack said. "There's nothing royal about all *this*." He pointed into a shattered dining room, where four grinning skeletons sat around a collapsed table, still waiting for their dinner. "Let's get to that pyramid for a better view."

Jack was relieved to find that the stepped sides of the pyramid made for very easy climbing. He scurried to the top like a squirrel and began to scan the city for something more 'royal.'

But then he was distracted by something else.

Jack's eyes popped when he looked out over the top of the jungle. The storm on the horizon was now pitch-black, like a vat of boiling tar in the sky. And it was heading directly for them. Spouts rose just offshore, whipping into the sky. It was only a matter of time before the storm would make landfall.

Jack stumbled quickly back down the pyramid, almost falling as he went.

"Storm. Coming. Huge," he panted, barely able to breathe.

"Like the one that nearly sank us all?" Fitzwilliam asked.

"Huger," Jack said, waving his arms excitedly. "Have to take cover. Winds . . ."

"Look!" Arabella shouted, pointing up one of the boulevards. It led straight to a huge, ruined, pyramid-shaped palace that was previously hidden from their view by the overgrown jungle that surrounded them. Its stone walls, once grand, were crumbling and strained. The vines that crawled up the

walls were twisting in the wind like venomous snakes.

"Well, looks like the very place one might find a cursed sword," Jack shouted back, holding his bandana against his head to keep it from blowing off.

Arabella nodded. "*And* a good place to take cover!"

Then a bolt of lightning shattered a stand of trees directly behind Jack. "To the palace!" he commanded.

CHAPTER NINE

The palace was a sight to behold. Even in its current, decrepit state, it had an aura of grandness. The doors, long since rotted off their hinges, revealed a formal hall that led to the rooms within.

Jack surveyed the entrance. They weren't going to be as well protected here as he had hoped. What had once been a solid, sturdy structure was now almost rocking in the storm. The wind howled through cracks in the boulders and bricks, and moaned down the hallways. It was difficult to see more than a few feet ahead or above through the gloom of the storm. Large sheets of spider-webs rippled in corners, and dead vines made eerie scratching noises on the floor.

Ornate trees and flowers were carved into the floor's giant flagstones. Rectangular, decorated warriors danced and fought. In the middle was a giant plaque of a god with a feathered headdress—Quetzalcoatl.

"I don't trust this," Tumen said, motioning toward a carving on the floor of the palace. "This is the mark of an Aztec god."

"Oh, good," Jack said. "That means we're on the right track!"

And then the floor fell away.

Tumen yelled and pitched into the giant pit that had opened up.

Fitzwilliam lunged forward and grabbed Tumen's arms. But the boy's weight and momentum was too much. Fitzwilliam slid over the floor and was pulled to the edge of the pit. Jack threw himself to the ground and grabbed Fitzwilliam's ankles.

It wasn't enough.

Jean grabbed onto Jack's legs, but they were all still being dragged toward the bottom of the pit. Jack's skin scraped against the flagstones. He tried to grind his feet into the floor, but it didn't help.

"I'm slipping!" Tumen cried.

One of his arms slipped out of Fitzwilliam's grasp. The sudden jerk pulled them all down another few feet. Fitzwilliam was yanked over the side. His face scraped against the ledge as he went, leaving a smear of blood on the stone.

Jean threw Constance aside—apologizing to her—and threw himself on top of Jack. But it still wasn't enough.

"Arabella!" Jack called out. "Rip off your skirt!"

"*What?*" she demanded, shocked.

"Just the outer one," he said in exasperation. "Tie it around that column and grab onto Jean!"

Without a second thought Arabella did as he said, tearing her outer skirt in as large a piece as possible. She then wrapped it around the base of a crumbled column and tied it back around her waist. She grabbed onto Jean.

Constance yowled unhelpfully.

Finally, their descent into the pit was stopped. Jack's head was over the edge, and he could see past Fitzwilliam and Tumen. Gleaming in the darkness below were what looked like giant, sharp spikes sticking out of foul-smelling black water.

"Bit of a close one, mate." Jack shivered.

Slowly, straining and groaning, the three

of them managed to pull Fitzwilliam out. And then Tumen, who was swearing profusely in whatever language he spoke.

With the floor opening up under them, the hall was now a wide black pit with narrow ledges on either side.

"I don't like heights," Jean said, looking nervously over the edge.

"I thought you were *monsieur* sailor extraordinaire," Fitzwilliam taunted.

"That's different!" Jean protested.

Jack, Arabella, and Tumen took one side and Jean, Fitzwilliam, and Constance the other. They kept their backs to the wall and moved slowly, edging one foot along at a time.

"Are those *alligators* down there?" Arabella said, hearing snaps in the black water below.

Jack looked down, and his eyes bulged.

"Don't look," he suggested, "or you'll wish they *were* alligators."

After what seemed like ages, they finally reached the other side of the pit.

"Well *that* was bloody awful," Fitzwilliam said, brushing a fleck of dust off his spotless jacket. Although his face was scratched from the edge of the pit, Fitz somehow didn't have a hair out of place.

"Jack, look," Arabella said.

In the room beyond, rows and rows of skeletons knelt, their bony faces toward the floor. And before them, seated in an enormous carved stone throne, was the grinning skeleton of Captain Stone-Eyed Sam.

CHAPTER TEN

*E*ven though there were no windows and the once-lit torches had rotted in their sockets, a ghostly bluish light illuminated the room.

Droplets of rain trickled through the areas where the grand marble ceiling had crumbled away, sprinkling the dead king and his subjects.

The pirate himself was still dressed in the richest fabrics, all rotted and full of holes. Velvet, silk, and the finest linen were now as worthless as Arabella's ruined skirt. A medallion of solid gold hung on a heavy chain around his neck. An orb of finely polished onyx filled his left eye socket—the stone that gave Stone-Eyed Sam his name. On his bony head was an elaborate pirate hat that managed to escape the perils of time. Its broad leather brim and feathers were all intact, and the captain still looked cocky in it.

Stone-Eyed Sam was a pirate king, even to the end. And most important, he had a really great hat.

"Everyone was right in the middle of something," Arabella said. "It's like they all dropped dead at once."

With Jack leading, the crew picked its way slowly through the skeletons. It was hard to avoid all of the bones. Something crunched under Arabella's foot; too late she realized it was the hand of an outstretched subject on the floor.

"Loyal to the last," Jack said, leaning down and looking directly into the skull's eye sockets. "Touching, really."

Arabella shivered as the group moved on to the throne.

Jack let out a strangled scream.

Everyone jumped and turned. Fitzwilliam reached for his sword.

"*Look*," Jack said in despair, pointing.

A rope hung in the shadows, one end leading up to the hole in the roof, where the rain was now pouring in. The other end of the rope hung in an elaborate knot directly over Stone-Eyed Sam on his throne.

And the pirate king himself was missing something very important.

"His left arm," Fitzwilliam realized. He turned to Arabella. Jack had already torn his

bandana off in frustration and thrown it to the ground. "You said that all the legends recall the Sword of Cortés clutched in Sam's left hand!"

"It's been ripped from his shoulder," Jean said, giving a low whistle. "Probably by whoever left this rope." He bent down to examine the dust on the throne.

"Whoever did this came very recently— and must have avoided the booby-trapped grand hall completely. He knew enough to come around the *back* way," Jack said, stamping his feet in frustration.

Jack ran a hand through his now bare and almost soaking wet hair and stomped over to Stone-Eyed Sam. He glared at the skeleton, which seemed to grin at him from underneath his leather tricorn. It really was kind of a fabulous hat, thought Jack, just the sort a powerful man *should* wear. . . .

Without a moment's hesitation, Jack swiped the flamboyantly plumed hat from the ivory skull and brushed it off, then popped it on his head.

"Jack! The man is *dead*," Fitzwilliam said disgustedly.

"It's the *least* he owes me, considering all the trouble we went through to get here," Jack said defensively. As soon as he could, he would find a mirror. He was pretty sure he looked dashing in his new hat.

"I can't *believe* this," Arabella said sadly, sitting down on the steps of the throne. All she had to look forward to now was her dad's temper and once again serving pints of ale to the slime of the earth at the Faithful Bride until marriage or death.

"It seemed so lucky, finding this island. As if we were already at the end of our quest," Fitzwilliam sighed. He tried to put on a brave face but couldn't hide his bitter disappointment. "I suppose it will be bananas and some horrid wife for me now."

Even Jean and Tumen weren't unaffected by the sorrow of their new friends. Constance mewed pitifully and Arabella, in her sadness, instinctively petted the cat behind the ear, before realizing what she was doing and pulling her hand quickly away.

Jack bent back over the dead pirate. Turning to make sure no one was looking, he slipped his finger into Sam's eye socket and pocketed the pirate's stone eye.

Then he noticed a dull and rusty glint under the captain's rotted lace collar.

Jack grinned and snapped the key he found there off its leather cord.

"There's one thing about kings and pirates, my lads . . . and lassie . . . and cat . . .

beast . . . thing," he said, holding the key up to show the others. "They both *love* treasure. And sword or not, I'll bet Stone-Eyed Sam had quite the haul hidden somewhere in this place."

Everyone's—even Constance's—eyes lit up at that.

An hour later, they had searched every room in the palace—including the dungeon and the treasure vaults, but they found nothing more than a few doubloons. They didn't even need the key. The wooden doors to the vaults had rotted away. There were some pretty lamps and old furniture and bolts of rotting silk in Captain Stone-Eyed Sam's bedroom—but nothing shiny, precious, and easy to carry.

"Someone has come already and cleaned this place out," Fitzwilliam observed.

"No, there's no footprints," Arabella

pointed out, "like there were around the throne room."

Jack frowned, thinking.

"Maybe this Sam was . . . allergic to treasure," Jean said, scratching Constance under the chin.

Jack's eyes lit up. "He was a pirate long *before* he was a king," he said.

"So?" Arabella asked, gathering around him. The others followed.

"So? Old habits are hard to break, Bell!" he said, his voice echoing in the royal bedroom. "Give me a hand with this," he ordered, pulling at the enormous ebony bed.

Jean and Fitzwilliam bent down to help. "What nonsense is this, Jack?" Fitzwilliam demanded. "We are not looking for his chamber pot, I hope."

Jack sighed in disgust while ripping up the small, rotted rug that was under the bed.

"You're not thinking like a pirate, Fitzy. When it comes to treasure, *trust no one*. And keep it close at hand. Believe me, I *know*," he added darkly.

He ran his hands over the floorboards and grinned when his fingers hit the groove that he was sure he would find. He blew a cloud of dust away and pointed at the keyhole in the door hidden in the floor. The key fit perfectly.

"Light me a torch, someone," Jack ordered, handing over his flint-and-tinder kit. Arabella and Tumen quickly did as he said.

He opened up the hatch and stuck his head down, holding the torch before him.

"Well?" Jean asked impatiently.

"Well," Jack said calmly, dropping the torch down into the blackness, "see for yourself."

Fitzwilliam, Arabella, Tumen, Jean, and

Constance crowded around eagerly. But it was Fitzwilliam who saw it first.

"By the King's blood . . ." he swore.

The torchlight flickered on what looked like a roomful of gold.

CHAPTER ELEVEN

Arabella sat, dazed, covered in jewelry. Ropes of pearls. Gold chains as thick as her thumb with ruby-encrusted pendants hanging from them. Bracelets studded with diamonds and emeralds. A small crown sat on her head, tipped sideways.

Normally, she wasn't into such girly things. But this was different. She had never before seen so much gold, so many beautiful things. Trinkets and baubles everywhere.

Goblets made out of carved crystal. Pretty little daggers in golden hilts with amethyst pommels. Chests overflowing with shiny yellow pieces of eight. Statues cast in solid, precious metals: dogs and jaguars and gods and birds of paradise. Constance lovingly rubbed up against a carved onyx cat with ruby eyes the size of plums.

Jack also draped some of the jewelry over himself; there was just no other way to carry it. All of the trunks and chests had rotted away, spilling their contents onto the ground. Only one was still good enough to carry out the treasure, and it was already full.

"All right, that's enough for the first trip," Jack decided, stuffing a few more rings into his pockets. "Let's load up, get it to the ship, and come back for the rest later."

Tumen laughed, watching Jean pose with

bracelets and a crown. "I thought this was going to be *un désastre*, washing up on this island," Jean admitted. "What an adventure—what *good* fortune—it has turned out to be!"

"Speaking of fortune—I shall not need my *father's* fortune now," Fitzwilliam murmured. He held a decorative sword made of pure gold. "He can disown me, for all I care. I shall return to England as my own man. . . ."

"I can do *whatever* I want," Arabella said, dreaming of the sort of freedom money could buy her. "I could buy my own tavern. Or a whole estate and be a lady of leisure!"

"I'm going to get myself some new clothes," Jean said. "And maybe my own ship."

"And a horse!" Tumen added.

"Now, wait a moment," Jack said, interrupting. "We'll do nothing with this treasure but finance our great quest—we still have to find the Sword of Cortés!"

Fitzwilliam and Arabella blinked, slowly remembering why they were there in the first place.

"What's so *great* about this sword?" Tumen asked. "She seems to get a lot of people killed."

"It has great power," Jack said, eyes glowing. "The power to cloud men's minds. The power to conquer empires. The power to forge kingdoms. This power can be ours. But more important, we can keep it out of the hands of the pirates that are searching for it. And maybe even rid ourselves of the pirates of the Caribbean once and for all. Then the seas will be free for *us* to rule!"

Everyone stared at him.

"Um, Jack. That last part? Ye're a little ambitious there?" Arabella said. Then, smiling, she continued, "I'm all for ambition."

"Agreed. It is a noble cause," Fitzwilliam decided. "I completely devote myself and my sword—" he looked at the useless golden decorative one in his hand, "my *other* sword—to avenging my sister."

Tumen and Jean looked at each other.

"I have worked on a merchant vessel ever since I was a child. I have been through enough pirate attacks for a lifetime," Jean said thoughtfully. "Sure, why not. Pirates are an evil lot," he said. Then he added: "But, the power and empire part? I like that, too."

"Beats hauling bananas around," Tumen said, shrugging.

"Then we're agreed. To the *Barnacle!*" Jack declared, grinning. It was all falling into place: the scabbard, the treasure, clues to the sword, and now a loyal crew.

They made a strange procession heading back out through the palace. Energized, the six of them marched through the dust and shadows, covered in jewels and carrying even more. The fierce wind in the halls didn't bother them half so much now, except when they had to walk against it with the heavy treasure in their hands. Even the spooky blue light and the rain in the throne room didn't dampen their spirits.

Jack took extra care guiding his end of the treasure chest around the throne. "Easy now. Don't want to disturb the dead . . . Hello, what's this?"

He dropped the chest—causing Fitzwilliam, who was carrying the other half, to fall on his rump. Jack had noticed something he hadn't seen before. He squatted to get a better look at the floor beneath the rope that hung from the ceiling.

The footprints Arabella had noticed were very strange indeed. "The fellow who took our fabled sword will have a lot of trouble running away with it. Look at this."

Everyone gathered around.

The prints were only of *left* feet—as if the man who made them had *two* of them.

"Left-Foot Louis!" Tumen and Jean shouted. They looked at each other in horror. Arabella blanched.

Before they could say anymore, a rumble and crackling came from above. The storm had broken a piece of the stony ceiling away. It fell into the crowd of kneeling skeletons. A flood of water poured through the now-huge hole in the ceiling, soaking everyone.

Constance hissed and yowled and hissed again, shaking herself like a dog.

"To the *Barnacle!*" Jack declared.

"Are ye *mad*?" Arabella said, shaking her hair out. "It's a disaster out there."

"She is right," Fitzwilliam agreed. "Let us wait it out in one of the other rooms, perhaps make a small fire for the night."

"Well, you lot do what you want then," Jack said, shrugging. He pulled up his sleeves and bent over to pick up the chest as best he could. "All of you may stay here among the crumbling ruins with the skeletons and the falling stones and the fearsome Captain Torrents. I, however, am taking myself, my ship, and this chest of gold, and getting out of here. Savvy?"

"Captain Torrents? What on earth are you talking . . ." Fitzwilliam began. Then he turned and saw the figure standing behind them. Tall. *Very* tall. With crazy gray eyes.

And very, very angry.

"To the *Barnacle!*" Arabella shouted. Jack rolled his eyes.

Fitzwilliam and Tumen together grabbed the other side of the chest, and Jean grabbed Constance. The six of them ran out, with Torrents right behind them.

CHAPTER TWELVE

*T*he driving wind and rain grew worse as the crew of the *Barnacle* ran through the palace. It beat down on them through the porous roof. They'd gotten a good head start on Torrents, but for every two steps they took, the giant only needed one, and he was gaining on them.

When they came to the hall with the carved stone floor—and the pit hidden underneath—Jack, Fitzwilliam, and Tumen skidded to a halt, barely stopping in time.

The trapdoors had closed again, but they all knew what lay beneath them.

"There's no way we can bring the chest, Jack!" Fitzwilliam shouted. "We'll have to leave it behind. We'll never be able to walk the ledges with it!"

"We are not going anywhere without the treasure!" Jack shouted back.

Torrents came around the far corner, a murderous look on his face.

"No, look. . . ." Arabella tapped on the floor with the golden scepter she was carrying. "The traps only work if you're trying to *get in*, not *out! Come on!*"

They picked up the chest and continued running. Torrents was at the far end of the room, and before the crew left the palace, Jack ran back across the floor.

"Jack!" Arabella called out as the trap opened once more.

Jack nimbly leapt back onto the ledge to rejoin his friends before the trap fully opened.

"Good luck getting around those narrow ledges, mate!" Jack called out to Torrents. "Let's go!" he barked at the crew.

Desperately scrambling, they managed to make it out of the palace and the city, through the jungle, and almost to the *Barnacle* before Fitzwilliam tripped over a driftwood log and dropped the chest.

Jack scrambled under the pouring sheets of rain to pick up the fallen coins. The surf was smashing against the shore and beating upon the beach as rain painfully pelted them. The storm was so strong that the crew was being tossed by the winds. Jean turned, trying to see through the driving rain to look for Torrents.

"Jack . . ." he yelled. "Look! He's made his way out of the palace!"

Torrents stood at the top of a nearby dune, roaring in anger. Over his head, terrible, dark clouds spiraled and boiled. Rain was pouring all around him. But not *on* him—he was completely dry in the eye of the storm. It was finally clear. The storm *was* following them, because *Torrents* had been following them! *He* was the eye of the storm, Jack realized with horror. The storm was coming *from* the pirate!

"Give me back the scabbard, boy! Or suffer the consequences!" Torrents snarled at Jack.

"What are your plans, mate? Drench me to death?" Jack asked, stepping between his friends and the pirate.

Torrents growled. As he grew angrier, the winds whipped even more fiercely around him. Hail suddenly began to pelt Jack's crew.

"Dock scum!" Torrents shouted. "If you don't fear me, which you'd be a fool not to—you will no doubt fear the power of the cursed Davy Jones!"

Jack laughed. "Oh, yes, Davy Jones. My fine Tortsy, Davy Jones is only a legend."

Torrents also laughed—but it was a brutal, sick laugh.

"I've *met* Davy Jones," the giant growled. "In the flesh. Consider yourself blessed that ye never had dealings with him who collects the souls of sailors and binds them to service before his ship. I was a 'guest' aboard his ship—maybe you've heard of it?—the *Flying Dutchman*." Arabella, Jean, Jack, and Tumen all shivered at the name. "Aye. The same terrible vessel whose very timbers are cut from the bodies and souls of doomed seamen. And I would have been doomed, too. But *I* was smart. *I* was able to make a deal with

Jones for my freedom. Now, I must find the Sword of Cortés and its scabbard, and bring them to Jones within one year's time or forever be bound to the *Dutchman*. He branded me, just so I wouldn't forget."

Torrents ripped open his shirt. Jack's eyes widened. On the pirate's chest, on scarred, blood-red tissue, was the feathered serpent— the same mark as on the scabbard of the Sword of Cortés.

"This mark *angered* the heathen gods, for they hate Cortés, and anything to do with him," Torrents continued, closing his shirt again. "They cursed me. Rain and storm wherever I go—worse when I've grown *angry*. And, my dear boy, right now, I'm very *very* angry."

There was a blast of thunder. The trees nearest Torrents were ripped out of the ground like weeds by the wind. Hail and rain hit like sharp glass. A static charge, like a blanket of lightning, covered the pirate's body. Sam's hat flew from Jack's head, and it was moments before he was able to sweep it up and put it back on.

Torrents strode toward the crew, glowing with lightning. The six shipmates backed down the beach, unable to look away. There was no way they could get into the *Barnacle*, if it had even survived the storm-churned surf. Behind them, the waves were the color of mud, crashing like a barrage of cannonballs upon the shore. Wind whipped a stinging, salty spray onto the crew, burning badly scraped and bruised skin. Jack had to keep blinking to be able to see at all.

Torrents continued to move forward, and the crew kept retreating. The pirate was going to force them into the stormy ocean—he was going to drown them!

Jean set one foot backward—and yelped when it landed in the surf. A heavy wave struck the crew members' backs. Lightning crackled around Torrents's head.

Arabella screamed and grabbed Fitzwilliam's arm. Tumen clutched Jean and Constance. Fitzwilliam drew his sword and made sure the others were behind him, but he didn't stop backing away.

Only Jack stood his ground defiantly.

Dry as firewood in the eye of the storm, Torrents reached for his sword. The air around him still snapped and popped with an electric charge.

Jack reached for his hat, which was now sopping wet, the brim filled with rain.

Jack took it off and calmly tossed the rain-water at Torrents.

There was a crackle and sputtering and hissing and finally a tremendous explosion.

Jack was thrown backward. Water and lightning were not a good mix—something most people wouldn't understand for quite some time. But Jack, of course, wasn't most people.

Torrents screamed in agony. Then he fell to the ground, unconscious, his body smoking.

"What has happened to him? How could mere water have such an effect on the devil himself? " Fitzwilliam demanded.

Jean and Tumen looked at each other in wonder.

Jack just smiled knowingly and mumbled quietly, "I told little Benny that trick I showed him with the kite and the key would someday prove useful. Just hope the lad remembers it as he gets older. Might do him some good, too."

"Look!" Arabella shouted, pointing to the shore. The storm was vanishing like vapor:

clouds pulled back, the wind died, and the sun shone—brighter than ever. Knocking Torrents unconscious had halted the storm. Miraculously, the *Barnacle* was still there, listing, but still afloat. Jack's decision to anchor just where he did had saved it from sinking.

The crew wasted no time heading out. While Arabella stowed the treasure and began bailing water below deck, the four boys worked on better securing the mast and sails. Constance walked around the ship, purring as if she owned it.

But as they sailed away, gray clouds began gathering again behind them. "Torrents must have woken up," Arabella murmured. Isla Esquelética was under a cover of clouds again, the storm growing black over its beaches and jungle. Another ship was also headed away from the island, in the other direction.

"That must be Torrents's ship," Jean said. "I suppose his crew mutinied."

"Well, that's it for him," Jack said, cheerfully. "Torrents is *never* getting off that island! The seas around it won't calm until his temper does, and we can wager our lives *that* will never happen."

"Hear, hear!" Arabella said with feeling, raising a silver goblet she'd found in the treasure room.

"All right then, lads!" Jack said, grinning. "You, Fitzy—haul up the main sail. Arabella, make secure that rigging over there. Tumen, try to figure out where in the blasted Caribbean we are. Jean, you take the wheel!"

"Where to, Jack?" Jean asked, grinning.

"Why, to find Left-Foot Louis, of course," Jack said, putting a foot up on the rail and looking out at the sea. He adjusted his hat. "And oh," he added as an afterthought,

"From now on, please remember . . .

"It's *Captain* Jack Sparrow!"

The *Barnacle* sailed on, and the crew was more determined than ever to acquire the Sword of Cortés for themselves. It would bring them power and freedom. And, now they knew, it would also keep them safe. After all, they would be keeping it out of the most dangerous hands on the seven seas—the barnacled claws of the cursed and feared Davy Jones.

We set sail for the closest port in Antigua to stock up on supplies, with Jumen and Jean navigating and setting our course. Those two really are a pair of excellent sailors. Meantime, we are closing in on the Sword, I can feel it. However, I am sorry to report that unfortunately, I've lost my fabulous hat to a trader on the docks of Isla Puerta in a wager over the ability of sea turtles to support human beings in open water. Still, with a ship as merry as the Barnacle and a crew as fierce as mine, I can imagine no obstacle great enough to stand in our way, not even the dreaded Left-Foot Louis. Mayhap the next entry in this Captain's log will be the tale of how we finally won the Sword of Cortés!

    —Captain Jack Sparrow

Don't miss the next volume in the continuing adventures of Jack Sparrow and the crew of the mighty Barnacle.

The Siren Song

The crew of the *Barnacle* has suddenly fallen under a sinister spell. While continuing their quest for the storied Sword of Cortés, the crew is entranced by an ethereal song and each of them attempts to take the *Barnacle* in a different direction—away from the sword's supposed location. Only Jack seems unaffected by the strange song, but can he both subdue his crew *and* defeat the mysterious force behind the dark spell?

Available now—wherever books are sold!